PENGUIN ARCHIVE

Do Not Go Gentle Into

GW01238449

Dylan Thomas

1914–1953

Dylan Thomas

Do Not Go Gentle Into That Good Night

PENGUIN ARCHIVE

PENGUIN BOOKS

UK | USA | Canada | Ireland | Australia
India | New Zealand | South Africa

Penguin Books is part of the Penguin Random House group of companies
whose addresses can be found at global.penguinrandomhouse.com

Penguin Random House UK,
One Embassy Gardens, 8 Viaduct Gardens, London SW11 7BW

penguin.co.uk

Dylan Thomas's *Collected Poems 1934–1952* published by J. M. Dent & Sons 1952
This edition published in Penguin Classics 2025

003

Set in 11.6/15 pt Dante MT Std
Typeset by Jouve (UK), Milton Keynes
Printed and bound in Great Britain by Clays Ltd, Elcograf S.p.A.

The authorized representative in the EEA is Penguin Random House Ireland,
Morrison Chambers, 32 Nassau Street, Dublin D02 YH68

A CIP catalogue record for this book is available from the British Library

ISBN: 978–0–241–74626–4

Penguin Random House is committed to a sustainable future
for our business, our readers and our planet. This book is made from
Forest Stewardship Council® certified paper.

Contents

Prologue   1

I have longed to move away   5

Why east wind chills   6

The hand that signed the paper   8

And death shall have no dominion   9

That sanity be kept   11

We lying by seasand   13

The force that through the green fuse   14

Before I knocked   16

When once the twilight locks   18

This bread I break   21

A process in the weather of the heart   22

Foster the light   24

I see the boys of summer   26

If I were tickled by the rub of love   29

Especially when the October wind   32

Should lanterns shine   34

After the funeral   35

The tombstone told   37

On no work of words   39

Once it was the colour of saying   40

If my head hurt a hair's foot   41

To Others than You   43

Paper and sticks   44

Into her lying down head   45

The Countryman's Return   48

Deaths and Entrances   52

Among those Killed in the Dawn Raid
      was a Man Aged a Hundred   54

Lie still, sleep becalmed   55

The conversation of prayers   56

A Winter's Tale   57

In my craft or sullen art   63

Fern Hill   64

In the White Giant's Thigh   67

Lament   70

This side of the truth   73

Do not go gentle into that good night   75

Prologue

This day winding down now
At God speeded summer's end
In the torrent salmon sun,
In my seashaken house
On a breakneck of rocks
Tangled with chirrup and fruit,
Froth, flute, fin and quill
At a wood's dancing hoof,
By scummed, starfish sands
With their fishwife cross
Gulls, pipers, cockles, and sails,
Out there, crow black, men
Tackled with clouds, who kneel
To the sunset nets,
Geese nearly in heaven, boys
Stabbing, and herons, and shells
That speak seven seas,
Eternal waters away
From the cities of nine
Days' night whose towers will catch
In the religious wind
Like stalks of tall, dry straw,
At poor peace I sing
To you, strangers, (though song

Is a burning and crested act,
The fire of birds in
The world's turning wood,
For my sawn, splay sounds),
Out of these seathumbed leaves
That will fly and fall
Like leaves of trees and as soon
Crumble and undie
Into the dogdayed night.
Seaward the salmon, sucked sun slips,
And the dumb swans drub blue
My dabbed bay's dusk, as I hack
This rumpus of shapes
For you to know
How I, a spinning man,
Glory also this star, bird
Roared, sea born, man torn, blood blest.
Hark: I trumpet the place,
From fish to jumping hill! Look:
I build my bellowing ark
To the best of my love
As the flood begins,
Out of the fountainhead
Of fear, rage red, manalive,
Molten and mountainous to stream
Over the wound asleep
Sheep white hollow farms

To Wales in my arms.
Hoo, there, in castle keep,
You king singsong owls, who moonbeam
The flickering runs and dive
The dingle furred deer dead!
Huloo, on plumbed bryns,
O my ruffled ring dove
In the hooting, nearly dark
With Welsh and reverent rook,
Coo rooing the woods' praise,
Who moons her blue notes from her nest
Down to the curlew herd!
Ho, hullaballoing clan
Agape, with woe
In your beaks, on the gabbing capes!
Heigh, on horseback hill, jack
Whisking hare! who
Hears, there, this fox light, my flood ship's
Clangour as I hew and smite
(A clash of anvils for my
Hubbub and fiddle, this tune
On a tongued puffball)
But animals thick as thieves
On God's rough tumbling grounds
(Hail to His beasthood!).
Beasts who sleep good and thin,
Hist, in hogsback woods! The haystacked
Hollow farms in a throng
Of waters cluck and cling,

And barnroofs cockcrow war!
O kingdom of neighbours, finned
Felled and quilled, flash to my patch
Work ark and the moonshine
Drinking Noah of the bay,
With pelt, and scale, and fleece:
Only the drowned deep bells
Of sheep and churches noise
Poor peace as the sun sets
And dark shoals every holy field.
We shall ride out alone, and then,
Under the stars of Wales,
Cry, Multitudes of arks! Across
The water lidded lands,
Manned with their loves they'll move,
Like wooden islands, hill to hill.
Huloo, my prowed dove with a flute!
Ahoy, old, sea-legged fox,
Tom tit and Dai mouse!
My ark sings in the sun
At God speeded summer's end
And the flood flowers now.

I have longed to move away

I have longed to move away
From the hissing of the spent lie
And the old terrors' continual cry
Growing more terrible as the day
Goes over the hill into the deep sea;
I have longed to move away
From the repetition of salutes,
For there are ghosts in the air
And ghostly echoes on paper,
And the thunder of calls and notes.

I have longed to move away but am afraid;
Some life, yet unspent, might explode
Out of the old lie burning on the ground,
And, crackling into the air, leave me half-blind.
Neither by night's ancient fear,
The parting of hat from hair,
Pursed lips at the receiver,
Shall I fall to death's feather.
By these I would not care to die,
Half convention and half lie.

Why east wind chills

Why east wind chills and south wind cools
Shall not be known till windwell dries
And west's no longer drowned
In winds that bring the fruit and rind
Of many a hundred falls;
Why silk is soft and the stone wounds
The child shall question all his days,
Why night-time rain and the breast's blood
Both quench his thirst he'll have a black reply.

When cometh Jack Frost? the children ask.
Shall they clasp a comet in their fists?
Not till, from high and low, their dust
Sprinkles in children's eyes a long-last sleep
And dusk is crowded with the children's ghosts,
Shall a white answer echo from the rooftops.

All things are known: the stars' advice
Calls some content to travel with the winds,
Though what the stars ask as they round
Time upon time the towers of the skies
Is heard but little till the stars go out.
I hear content, and 'Be content'
Ring like a handbell through the corridors,

And 'Know no answer,' and I know
No answer to the children's cry
Of echo's answer and the man of frost
And ghostly comets over the raised fists.

The hand that signed the paper

The hand that signed the paper felled a city;
Five sovereign fingers taxed the breath,
Doubled the globe of dead and halved a country;
These five kings did a king to death.

The mighty hand leads to a sloping shoulder,
The finger joints are cramped with chalk;
A goose's quill has put an end to murder
That put an end to talk.

The hand that signed the treaty bred a fever,
And famine grew, and locusts came;
Great is the hand that holds dominion over
Man by a scribbled name.

The five kings count the dead, but do not soften
The crusted wound nor stroke the brow;
A hand rules pity as a hand rules heaven;
Hands have no tears to flow.

And death shall have no dominion

And death shall have no dominion.
Dead men naked they shall be one
With the man in the wind and the west moon;
When their bones are picked clean and the clean bones gone,
They shall have stars at elbow and foot;
Though they go mad they shall be sane,
Though they sink through the sea they shall rise again;
Though lovers be lost love shall not;
And death shall have no dominion.

And death shall have no dominion.
Under the windings of the sea
They lying long shall not die windily;
Twisting on racks when sinews give way,
Strapped to a wheel, yet they shall not break;
Faith in their hands shall snap in two,
And the unicorn evils run them through;
Split all ends up they shan't crack;
And death shall have no dominion.

And death shall have no dominion,
No more may gulls cry at their ears
Or waves break loud on the seashores;
Where blew a flower may a flower no more

Lift its head to the blows of the rain;
Though they be mad and dead as nails,
Heads of the characters hammer through daisies;
Break in the sun till the sun breaks down,
And death shall have no dominion.

That sanity be kept

That sanity be kept I sit at open windows,
Regard the sky, make unobtrusive comment on the moon,
Sit at open windows in my shirt,
And let the traffic pass, the signals shine,
The engines run, the brass bands keep in tune,
For sanity must be preserved.

Thinking of death, I sit and watch the park
Where children play in all their innocence,
And matrons, on the littered grass,
Absorb the daily sun.

The sweet suburban music from a hundred lawns
Comes softly to my ears. The English mowers mow and mow.

I mark the couples walking arm in arm,
Observe their smiles,
Sweet invitations and inventions,
See them lend love illustration
By gesture and grimace.
I watch them curiously, detect beneath the laughs
What stands for grief, a vague bewilderment
At things not turning right.

I sit at open windows in my shirt,
Observe, like some Jehovah of the west,
What passes by, that sanity be kept.

We lying by seasand

We lying by seasand, watching yellow
And the grave sea, mock who deride
Who follow the red rivers, hollow
Alcove of words out of cicada shade,
For in this yellow grave of sand and sea
A calling for colour calls with the wind
That's grave and gay as grave and sea
Sleeping on either hand.
The lunar silences, the silent tide
Lapping the still canals, the dry tide-master
Ribbed between desert and water storm,
Should cure our ills of the water
With a one-coloured calm;
The heavenly music over the sand
Sounds with the grains as they hurry
Hiding the golden mountains and mansions
Of the grave, gay, seaside land.
Bound by a sovereign strip, we lie,
Watch yellow, wish for wind to blow away
The strata of the shore and drown red rock;
But wishes breed not, neither
Can we fend off rock arrival,
Lie watching yellow until the golden weather
Breaks, O my heart's blood, like a heart and hill.

The force that through the green fuse

The force that through the green fuse drives the flower
Drives my green age; that blasts the roots of trees
Is my destroyer.
And I am dumb to tell the crooked rose
My youth is bent by the same wintry fever.

The force that drives the water through the rocks
Drives my red blood; that dries the mouthing streams
Turns mine to wax.
And I am dumb to mouth unto my veins
How at the mountain spring the same mouth sucks.

The hand that whirls the water in the pool
Stirs the quicksand; that ropes the blowing wind
Hauls my shroud sail.
And I am dumb to tell the hanging man
How of my clay is made the hangman's lime.

The lips of time leech to the fountain head;
Love drips and gathers, but the fallen blood
Shall calm her sores.

And I am dumb to tell a weather's wind
How time has ticked a heaven round the stars.

And I am dumb to tell the lover's tomb
How at my sheet goes the same crooked worm.

Before I knocked

Before I knocked and flesh let enter,
With liquid hands tapped on the womb,
I who was shapeless as the water
That shaped the Jordan near my home
Was brother to Mnetha's daughter
And sister to the fathering worm.

I who was deaf to spring and summer,
Who knew not sun nor moon by name,
Felt thud beneath my flesh's armour,
As yet was in a molten form,
The leaden stars, the rainy hammer
Swung by my father from his dome.

I knew the message of the winter,
The darted hail, the childish snow,
And the wind was my sister suitor;
Wind in me leaped, the hellborn dew;
My veins flowed with the Eastern weather;
Ungotten I knew night and day.

As yet ungotten, I did suffer,
The rack of dreams my lily bones
Did twist into a living cipher,

And flesh was snipped to cross the lines
Of gallow crosses on the liver
And brambles in the wringing brains.

My throat knew thirst before the structure
Of skin and vein around the well
Where words and water make a mixture
Unfailing till the blood runs foul;
My heart knew love, my belly hunger;
I smelt the maggot in my stool.

And time cast forth my mortal creature
To drift or drown upon the seas
Acquainted with the salt adventure
Of tides that never touch the shores.
I who was rich was made the richer
By sipping at the vine of days.

I, born of flesh and ghost, was neither
A ghost nor man, but mortal ghost.
And I was struck down by death's feather.
I was mortal to the last
Long breath that carried to my father
The message of his dying christ.

You who bow down at cross and altar,
Remember me and pity Him
Who took my flesh and bone for armour
And doublecrossed my mother's womb.

When once the twilight locks

When once the twilight locks no longer
Locked in the long worm of my finger
Nor dammed the sea that sped about my fist,
The mouth of time sucked, like a sponge,
The milky acid on each hinge,
And swallowed dry the waters of the breast.

When the galactic sea was sucked
And all the dry seabed unlocked,
I sent my creature scouting on the globe,
That globe itself of hair and bone
That, sewn to me by nerve and brain,
Had stringed my flask of matter to his rib.

My fuses timed to charge his heart,
He blew like powder to the light
And held a little sabbath with the sun,
But when the stars, assuming shape,
Drew in his eyes the straws of sleep,
He drowned his father's magics in a dream.

All issue armoured, of the grave,
The redhaired cancer still alive,
The cataracted eyes that filmed their cloth;
Some dead undid their bushy jaws,
And bags of blood let out their flies;
He had by heart the Christ-cross-row of death.

Sleep navigates the tides of time;
The dry Sargasso of the tomb
Gives up its dead to such a working sea;
And sleep rolls mute above the beds
Where fishes' food is fed the shades
Who periscope through flowers to the sky.

The hanged who lever from the limes
Ghostly propellers for their limbs,
The cypress lads who wither with the cock,
These, and the others in sleep's acres,
Of dreaming men make moony suckers,
And snipe the fools of vision in the back.

When once the twilight screws were turned,
And mother milk was stiff as sand,
I sent my own ambassador to light;
By trick or chance he fell asleep
And conjured up a carcase shape
To rob me of my fluids in his heart.

Awake, my sleeper, to the sun,
A worker in the morning town,
And leave the poppied pickthank where he lies;
The fences of the light are down,
All but the briskest riders thrown,
And worlds hang on the trees.

This bread I break

This bread I break was once the oat,
This wine upon a foreign tree
Plunged in its fruit;
Man in the day or wind at night
Laid the crops low, broke the grape's joy.

Once in this wine the summer blood
Knocked in the flesh that decked the vine,
Once in this bread
The oat was merry in the wind;
Man broke the sun, pulled the wind down.

This flesh you break, this blood you let
Make desolation in the vein,
Were oat and grape
Born of the sensual root and sap;
My wine you drink, my bread you snap.

A process in the weather of the heart

A process in the weather of the heart
Turns damp to dry; the golden shot
Storms in the freezing tomb.
A weather in the quarter of the veins
Turns night to day; blood in their suns
Lights up the living worm.

A process in the eye forwarns
The bones of blindness; and the womb
Drives in a death as life leaks out.

A darkness in the weather of the eye
Is half its light; the fathomed sea
Breaks on unangled land.
The seed that makes a forest of the loin
Forks half its fruit; and half drops down,
Slow in a sleeping wind.

A weather in the flesh and bone
Is damp and dry; the quick and dead
Move like two ghosts before the eye.

A process in the weather of the world
Turns ghost to ghost; each mothered child
Sits in their double shade.
A process blows the moon into the sun,
Pulls down the shabby curtains of the skin;
And the heart gives up its dead.

Foster the light

Foster the light nor veil the manshaped moon,
Nor weather winds that blow not down the bone,
But strip the twelve-winded marrow from his circle;
Master the night nor serve the snowman's brain
That shapes each bushy item of the air
Into a polestar pointed on an icicle.

Murmur of spring nor crush the cockerel's eggs,
Nor hammer back a season in the figs,
But graft these four-fruited ridings on your country;
Farmer in time of frost the burning leagues,
By red-eyed orchards sow the seeds of snow,
In your young years the vegetable century.

And father all nor fail the fly-lord's acre,
Nor sprout on owl-seed like a goblin-sucker,
But rail with your wizard's ribs the heart-shaped planet;
Of mortal voices to the ninnies' choir,
High lord esquire, speak up the singing cloud,
And pluck a mandrake music from the marrowroot.

Roll unmanly over this turning tuft,
O ring of seas, nor sorrow as I shift
From all my mortal lovers with a starboard smile;

Nor when my love lies in the cross-boned drift
Naked among the bow-and-arrow birds
Shall you turn cockwise on a tufted axle.

Who gave these seas their colour in a shape
Shaped my clayfellow, and the heaven's ark
In time at flood filled with his coloured doubles;
O who is glory in the shapeless maps,
Now make the world of me as I have made
A merry manshape of your walking circle.

I see the boys of summer

I

I see the boys of summer in their ruin
Lay the gold tithings barren,
Setting no store by harvest, freeze the soils;
There in their heat the winter floods
Of frozen loves they fetch their girls,
And drown the cargoed apples in their tides.

These boys of light are curdlers in their folly,
Sour the boiling honey;
The jacks of frost they finger in the hives;
There in the sun the frigid threads
Of doubt and dark they feed their nerves;
The signal moon is zero in their voids.

I see the summer children in their mothers
Split up the brawned womb's weathers,
Divide the night and day with fairy thumbs;
There in the deep with quartered shades
Of sun and moon they paint their dams
As sunlight paints the shelling of their heads.

I see that from these boys shall men of nothing
Stature by seeding shifting,
Or lame the air with leaping from its heats;
There from their hearts the dogdayed pulse
Of love and light bursts in their throats.
O see the pulse of summer in the ice.

II

But seasons must be challenged or they totter
Into a chiming quarter
Where, punctual as death, we ring the stars;
There, in his night, the black-tongued bells
The sleepy man of winter pulls,
Nor blows back moon-and-midnight as she blows.

We are the dark deniers, let us summon
Death from a summer woman,
A muscling life from lovers in their cramp,
From the fair dead who flush the sea
The bright-eyed worm on Davy's lamp,
And from the planted womb the man of straw.

We summer boys in this four-winded spinning,
Green of the seaweeds' iron,
Hold up the noisy sea and drop her birds,
Pick the world's ball of wave and froth

To choke the deserts with her tides,
And comb the county gardens for a wreath.

In spring we cross our foreheads with the holly,
Heigh ho the blood and berry,
And nail the merry squires to the trees;
Here love's damp muscle dries and dies,
Here break a kiss in no love's quarry.
O see the poles of promise in the boys.

III

I see you boys of summer in your ruin.
Man in his maggot's barren.
And boys are full and foreign in the pouch.
I am the man your father was.
We are the sons of flint and pitch.
O see the poles are kissing as they cross.

If I were tickled by the rub of love

If I were tickled by the rub of love,
A rooking girl who stole me for her side,
Broke through her straws, breaking my bandaged string,
If the red tickle as the cattle calve
Still set to scratch a laughter from my lung,
I would not fear the apple nor the flood
Nor the bad blood of spring.

Shall it be male or female? say the cells,
And drop the plum like fire from the flesh.
If I were tickled by the hatching hair,
The winging bone that sprouted in the heels,
The itch of man upon the baby's thigh,
I would not fear the gallows nor the axe
Nor the crossed sticks of war.

Shall it be male or female? say the fingers
That chalk the walls with green girls and their men.
I would not fear the muscling-in of love
If I were tickled by the urchin hungers
Rehearsing heat upon a raw-edged nerve.
I would not fear the devil in the loin
Nor the outspoken grave.

If I were tickled by the lovers' rub
That wipes away not crow's-foot nor the lock
Of sick old manhood on the fallen jaws,
Time and the crabs and the sweethearting crib
Would leave me cold as butter for the flies,
The sea of scums could drown me as it broke
Dead on the sweethearts' toes.

This world is half the devil's and my own,
Daft with the drug that's smoking in a girl
And curling round the bud that forks her eye.
An old man's shank one-marrowed with my bone,
And all the herrings smelling in the sea,
I sit and watch the worm beneath my nail
Wearing the quick away.

And that's the rub, the only rub that tickles.
The knobbly ape that swings along his sex
From damp love-darkness and the nurse's twist
Can never raise the midnight of a chuckle,
Nor when he finds a beauty in the breast
Of lover, mother, lovers, or his six
Feet in the rubbing dust.

And what's the rub? Death's feather on the nerve?
Your mouth, my love, the thistle in the kiss?
My Jack of Christ born thorny on the tree?
The words of death are dryer than his stiff,

My wordy wounds are printed with your hair.
I would be tickled by the rub that is:
Man be my metaphor.

Especially when the October wind

Especially when the October wind
With frosty fingers punishes my hair,
Caught by the crabbing sun I walk on fire
And cast a shadow crab upon the land,
By the sea's side, hearing the noise of birds,
Hearing the raven cough in winter sticks,
My busy heart who shudders as she talks
Sheds the syllabic blood and drains her words.

Shut, too, in a tower of words, I mark
On the horizon walking like the trees
The wordy shapes of women, and the rows
Of the star-gestured children in the park.
Some let me make you of the vowelled beeches,
Some of the oaken voices, from the roots
Of many a thorny shire tell you notes,
Some let me make you of the water's speeches.

Behind a pot of ferns the wagging clock
Tells me the hour's word, the neural meaning
Flies on the shafted disc, declaims the morning
And tells the windy weather in the cock.
Some let me make you of the meadow's signs;

The signal grass that tells me all I know
Breaks with the wormy winter through the eye.
Some let me tell you of the raven's sins.

Especially when the October wind
(Some let me make you of autumnal spells,
The spider-tongued, and the loud hill of Wales)
With fist of turnips punishes the land,
Some let me make you of the heartless words.
The heart is drained that, spelling in the scurry
Of chemic blood, warned of the coming fury.
By the sea's side hear the dark-vowelled birds.

Should lanterns shine

Should lanterns shine, the holy face,
Caught in an octagon of unaccustomed light,
Would wither up, and any boy of love
Look twice before he fell from grace.
The features in their private dark
Are formed of flesh, but let the false day come
And from her lips the faded pigments fall,
The mummy cloths expose an ancient breast.

I have been told to reason by the heart,
But heart, like head, leads helplessly;
I have been told to reason by the pulse,
And, when it quickens, alter the actions' pace
Till field and roof lie level and the same
So fast I move defying time, the quiet gentleman
Whose beard wags in Egyptian wind.
I have heard many years of telling,
And many years should see some change.

The ball I threw while playing in the park
Has not yet reached the ground.

After the funeral

(In memory of Ann Jones)

After the funeral, mule praises, brays,
Windshake of sailshaped ears, muffle-toed tap
Tap happily of one peg in the thick
Grave's foot, blinds down the lids, the teeth in black,
The spittled eyes, the salt ponds in the sleeves,
Morning smack of the spade that wakes up sleep,
Shakes a desolate boy who slits his throat
In the dark of the coffin and sheds dry leaves,
That breaks one bone to light with a judgment clout,
After the feast of tear-stuffed time and thistles
In a room with a stuffed fox and a stale fern,
I stand, for this memorial's sake, alone
In the snivelling hours with dead, humped Ann
Whose hooded, fountain heart once fell in puddles
Round the parched worlds of Wales and drowned each sun
(Though this for her is a monstrous image blindly
Magnified out of praise; her death was a still drop;
She would not have me sinking in the holy
Flood of her heart's fame; she would lie dumb and deep
And need no druid of her broken body).
But I, Ann's bard on a raised hearth, call all
The seas to service that her wood-tongued virtue

Babble like a bellbuoy over the hymning heads,
Bow down the walls of the ferned and foxy woods
That her love sing and swing through a brown chapel,
Bless her bent spirit with four, crossing birds.
Her flesh was meek as milk, but this skyward statue
With the wild breast and blessed and giant skull
Is carved from her in a room with a wet window
In a fiercely mourning house in a crooked year.
I know her scrubbed and sour humble hands
Lie with religion in their cramp, her threadbare
Whisper in a damp word, her wits drilled hollow,
Her fist of a face died clenched on a round pain;
And sculptured Ann is seventy years of stone.
These cloud-sopped, marble hands, this monumental
Argument of the hewn voice, gesture and psalm
Storm me forever over her grave until
The stuffed lung of the fox twitch and cry Love
And the strutting fern lay seeds on the black sill.

The tombstone told

The tombstone told when she died.
Her two surnames stopped me still.
A virgin married at rest.
She married in this pouring place,
That I struck one day by luck,
Before I heard in my mother's side
Or saw in the looking-glass shell
The rain through her cold heart speak
And the sun killed in her face.
More the thick stone cannot tell.

Before she lay on a stranger's bed
With a hand plunged through her hair,
Or that rainy tongue beat back
Through the devilish years and innocent deaths
To the room of a secret child,
Among men later I heard it said
She cried her white-dressed limbs were bare
And her red lips were kissed black,
She wept in her pain and made mouths,
Talked and tore though her eyes smiled.

I who saw in a hurried film
Death and this mad heroine
Meet once on a mortal wall
Heard her speak through the chipped beak
Of the stone bird guarding her:
I died before bedtime came
But my womb was bellowing
And I felt with my bare fall
A blazing red harsh head tear up
And the dear floods of his hair.

On no work of words

On no work of words now for three lean months in the bloody
Belly of the rich year and the big purse of my body
I bitterly take to task my poverty and craft:

To take to give is all, return what is hungrily given
Puffing the pounds of manna up through the dew to heaven,
The lovely gift of the gab bangs back on a blind shaft.

To lift to leave from the treasures of man is pleasing death
That will rake at last all currencies of the marked breath
And count the taken, forsaken mysteries in a bad dark.

To surrender now is to pay the expensive ogre twice.
Ancient woods of my blood, dash down to the nut of the seas
If I take to burn or return this world which is each man's work.

Once it was the colour of saying

Once it was the colour of saying
Soaked my table the uglier side of a hill
With a capsized field where a school sat still
And a black and white patch of girls grew playing;
The gentle seaslides of saying I must undo
That all the charmingly drowned arise to cockcrow and kill.
When I whistled with mitching boys through a reservoir park
Where at night we stoned the cold and cuckoo
Lovers in the dirt of their leafy beds,
The shade of their trees was a word of many shades
And a lamp of lightning for the poor in the dark;
Now my saying shall be my undoing,
And every stone I wind off like a reel.

If my head hurt a hair's foot

'If my head hurt a hair's foot
Pack back the downed bone. If the unpricked ball of my breath
Bump on a spout let the bubbles jump out.
Sooner drop with the worm of the ropes round my throat
Than bully ill love in the clouted scene.

All game phrases fit your ring of a cockfight:
I'll comb the snared woods with a glove on a lamp,
Peck, sprint, dance on fountains and duck time
Before I rush in a crouch the ghost with a hammer, air,
Strike light, and bloody a loud room.

If my bunched, monkey coming is cruel
Rage me back to the making house. My hand unravel
When you sew the deep door. The bed is a cross place.
Bend, if my journey ache, direction like an arc or make
A limp and riderless shape to leap nine thinning months.'

'No. Not for Christ's dazzling bed
Or a nacreous sleep among soft particles and charms
My dear would I change my tears or your iron head.
Thrust, my daughter or son, to escape, there is none, none, none,
Nor when all ponderous heaven's host of waters breaks.

Now to awake hushed of gestures and my joy like a cave
To the anguish and carrion, to the infant forever unfree,
O my lost love bounced from a good home;
The grain that hurries this way from the rim of the grave
Has a voice and a house, and there and here you must couch
    and cry.

Rest beyond choice in the dust-appointed grain,
At the breast stored with seas. No return
Through the waves of the fat streets nor the skeleton's thin ways.
The grave and my calm body are shut to your coming as stone,
And the endless beginning of prodigies suffers open.'

To Others than You

Friend by enemy I call you out.

You with a bad coin in your socket,
You my friend there with a winning air
Who palmed the lie on me when you looked
Brassily at my shyest secret,
Enticed with twinkling bits of the eye
Till the sweet tooth of my love bit dry,
Rasped at last, and I stumbled and sucked,
Whom now I conjure to stand as thief
In the memory worked by mirrors,
With unforgettably smiling act,
Quickness of hand in the velvet glove
And my whole heart under your hammer,
Were once such a creature, so gay and frank
A desireless familiar
I never thought to utter or think
While you displaced a truth in the air,

That though I loved them for their faults
As much as for their good,
My friends were enemies on stilts
With their heads in a cunning cloud.

Paper and sticks

Paper and sticks and shovel and match
Why won't the news of the old world catch
And the fire in a temper start

Once I had a rich boy for myself
I loved his body and his navy blue wealth
And I lived in his purse and his heart

When in our bed I was tossing and turning
All I could see were his brown eyes burning
By the green of a one pound note

I talk to him as I clean the grate
O my dear it's never too late
To take me away as you whispered and wrote

I had a handsome and well-off boy
I'll share my money and we'll run for joy
With a bouncing and silver spooned kid

Sharp and shrill my silly tongue scratches
Words on the air as the fire catches
You never did and *he* never did.

Into her lying down head

I

Into her lying down head
His enemies entered bed,
Under the encumbered eyelid,
Through the rippled drum of the hair-buried ear;
And Noah's rekindled now unkind dove
Flew man-bearing there.
Last night in a raping wave
Whales unreined from the green grave
In fountains of origin gave up their love,
Along her innocence glided
Juan aflame and savagely young King Lear,
Queen Catherine howling bare
And Samson drowned in his hair,
The colossal intimacies of silent
Once seen strangers or shades on a stair;
There the dark blade and wanton sighing her down
To a haycock couch and the scythes of his arms
Rode and whistled a hundred times
Before the crowing morning climbed;
Man was the burning England she was sleep-walking, and the
enamouring island
Made her limbs by luminous charms,

45

Sleep to a newborn sleep in a swaddling loin-leaf stroked
   and sang
        And his runaway beloved childlike laid in the
        acorned sand.

II

        There where a numberless tongue
        Wound their room with a male moan,
    His faith around her flew undone
And darkness hung the walls with baskets of snakes,
A furnace-nostrilled column-membered
           Super-or-near man
        Resembling to her dulled sense
        The thief of adolescence,
Early imaginary half remembered
        Oceanic lover alone
Jealously cannot forget for all her sakes,
        Made his bad bed in her good
        Night, and enjoyed as he would.
Crying, white gowned, from the middle moonlit stages
        Out to the tiered and hearing tide,
Close and far she announced the theft of the heart
In the taken body at many ages,
        Trespasser and broken bride
        Celebrating at her side
All blood-signed assailings and vanished marriages in which he
   had no lovely part
    Nor could share, for his pride, to the least

Mutter and foul wingbeat of the solemnizing nightpriest
Her holy unholy hours with the always anonymous beast.

III

Two sand grains together in bed,
Head to heaven-circling head,
Singly lie with the whole wide shore,
The covering sea their nightfall with no names;
And out of every domed and soil-based shell
One voice in chains declaims
The female, deadly, and male
Libidinous betrayal,
Golden dissolving under the water veil.
A she bird sleeping brittle by
Her lover's wings that fold tomorrow's flight,
Within the nested treefork
Sings to the treading hawk
Carrion, paradise, chirrup my bright yolk.
A blade of grass longs with the meadow,
A stone lies lost and locked in the lark-high hill.
Open as to the air to the naked shadow
O she lies alone and still,
Innocent between two wars,
With the incestuous secret brother in the seconds to
perpetuate the stars,
A man torn up mourns in the sole night.
And the second comers, the severers, the enemies from the deep
Forgotten dark, rest their pulse and bury their dead in her
faithless sleep.

The Countryman's Return

Embracing low-falutin
London (said the odd man in
A country pot, his hutch in
The fields, by a motherlike henrun)
With my fishtail hands and gently
Manuring popeye or
Swelling in flea-specked linen
The rankest of the city
I spent my unwasteable
Time among walking pintables
With sprung and padded shoulders,
Tomorrow's drunk club majors
Growing their wounds already,
The last war's professional
Unclaimed dead, girls from good homes
Studying the testicle
In communal crab flats
With the Sunflowers laid on,
Old paint-stained tumblers riding
On stools to a one man show down,
Gasketted and sirensuited
Bored and viciously waiting
Nightingales of the casualty stations

In the afternoon wasters
White feathering the living.

London's arches are falling
In, in Pedro's or Wendy's
With a silverfox farmer
Trying his hand at failing
Again, a collected poet
And some dismantled women,
Razor man and belly king,
I propped humanity's weight
Against the fruit machine,
Opened my breast and into
The spongebag let them all melt.
Zip once more for a traveller
With his goods under his eyes,
Another with hers under her belt,
The black man bleached to his tide
Mark, trumpet lipped and blackhead
Eyed, while the tears drag on the tail,
The weighing-scales, of my hand.
Then into blind streets I swam
Alone with my bouncing bag,
Too full to bow to the dim
Moon with a relation's face
Or lift my hat to unseen
Brothers dodging through the fog
The affectionate pickpocket
And childish, snivelling queen.

Beggars, robbers, inveiglers,
Voices from manholes and drains,
Maternal short time pieces,
Octopuses in doorways,
Dark inviters to keyholes
And evenings with great danes,
Bedsitting girls on the beat
With nothing for the metre,
Others whose single beds hold two
Only to make two ends meet,
All the hypnotised city's
Insidious procession
Hawking for money and pity
Among the hardly possessed.
And I in the wanting sway
Caught among never enough

Conjured me to resemble
A singing Walt from the mower
And jerrystone trim villas
Of the upper of the lower half,
Beardlessly wagging in Dean Street,
Blessing and counting the bustling
Twolegged handbagged sparrows,
Flogging into the porches
My cavernous, featherbed self.

Cut. Cut the crushed streets, leaving
A hole of errands and shades;

Plug the paper-blowing tubes;
Emasculate the seedy clocks;
Rub off the scrawl of prints on
Body and air and building;
Branch and leaf the birdless roofs;
Faces of melting visions,
Magdalene prostitution,
Glamour of the bloodily bowed,
Exaltation of the blind,
That sin-embracing dripper of fun
Sweep away like a cream cloud;
Bury all rubbish and love signs
Of my week in the dirtbox
In this anachronistic scene
Where sitting in clean linen
In a hutch in a cowpatched glen
Now I delight, I suppose, in
The countryman's return
And count by birds' eggs and leaves
The rusticating minutes,
The wasteful hushes among trees.
And O to cut the green field, leaving
One rich street with hunger in it.

Deaths and Entrances

On almost the incendiary eve
    Of several near deaths,
When one at the great least of your best loved
    And always known must leave
Lions and fires of his flying breath,
    Of your immortal friends
Who'd raise the organs of the counted dust
    To shoot and sing your praise,
One who called deepest down shall hold his peace
    That cannot sink or cease
    Endlessly to his wound
In many married London's estranging grief.

On almost the incendiary eve
    When at your lips and keys,
Locking, unlocking, the murdered strangers weave,
    One who is most unknown,
Your polestar neighbour, sun of another street,
    Will dive up to his tears.
He'll bathe his raining blood in the male sea
    Who strode for your own dead
And wind his globe out of your water thread

And load the throats of shells
    With every cry since light
Flashed first across his thunderclapping eyes.

On almost the incendiary eve
    Of deaths and entrances,
When near and strange wounded on London's waves
    Have sought your single grave,
One enemy, of many, who knows well
    Your heart is luminous
In the watched dark, quivering through locks and caves,
    Will pull the thunderbolts
To shut the sun, plunge, mount your darkened keys
    And sear just riders back,
    Until that one loved least
Looms the last Samson of your zodiac.

Among those Killed in the Dawn Raid was a Man Aged a Hundred

When the morning was waking over the war
He put on his clothes and stepped out and he died,
The locks yawned loose and a blast blew them wide,
He dropped where he loved on the burst pavement stone
And the funeral grains of the slaughtered floor.
Tell his street on its back he stopped a sun
And the craters of his eyes grew springshoots and fire
When all the keys shot from the locks, and rang.
Dig no more for the chains of his grey-haired heart.
The heavenly ambulance drawn by a wound
Assembling waits for the spade's ring on the cage.
O keep his bones away from that common cart,
The morning is flying on the wings of his age
And a hundred storks perch on the sun's right hand.

Lie still, sleep becalmed

Lie still, sleep becalmed, sufferer with the wound
In the throat, burning and turning. All night afloat
On the silent sea we have heard the sound
That came from the wound wrapped in the salt sheet.

Under the mile off moon we trembled listening
To the sea sound flowing like blood from the loud wound
And when the salt sheet broke in a storm of singing
The voices of all the drowned swam on the wind.

Open a pathway through the slow sad sail,
Throw wide to the wind the gates of the wandering boat
For my voyage to begin to the end of my wound,
We heard the sea sound sing, we saw the salt sheet tell.
Lie still, sleep becalmed, hide the mouth in the throat,
Or we shall obey, and ride with you through the drowned.

The conversation of prayers

The conversation of prayers about to be said
By the child going to bed and the man on the stairs
Who climbs to his dying love in her high room,
The one not caring to whom in his sleep he will move
And the other full of tears that she will be dead,

Turns in the dark on the sound they know will arise
Into the answering skies from the green ground,
From the man on the stairs and the child by his bed.
The sound about to be said in the two prayers
For the sleep in a safe land and the love who dies

Will be the same grief flying. Whom shall they calm?
Shall the child sleep unharmed or the man be crying?
The conversation of prayers about to be said
Turns on the quick and the dead, and the man on the stairs
Tonight shall find no dying but alive and warm

In the fire of his care his love in the high room.
And the child not caring to whom he climbs his prayer
Shall drown in a grief as deep as his true grave,
And mark the dark eyed wave, through the eyes of sleep,
Dragging him up the stairs to one who lies dead.

A Winter's Tale

It is a winter's tale
That the snow blind twilight ferries over the lakes
And floating fields from the farm in the cup of the vales,
Gliding windless through the hand folded flakes,
The pale breath of cattle at the stealthy sail,

And the stars falling cold,
And the smell of hay in the snow, and the far owl
Warning among the folds, and the frozen hold
Flocked with the sheep white smoke of the farm house cowl
In the river wended vales where the tale was told.

Once when the world turned old
On a star of faith pure as the drifting bread,
As the food and flames of the snow, a man unrolled
The scrolls of fire that burned in his heart and head,
Torn and alone in a farm house in a fold

Of fields. And burning then
In his firelit island ringed by the winged snow
And the dung hills white as wool and the hen
Roosts sleeping chill till the flame of the cock crow
Combs through the mantled yards and the morning men

Stumble out with their spades,
The cattle stirring, the mousing cat stepping shy,
The puffed birds hopping and hunting, the milk maids
Gentle in their clogs over the fallen sky,
And all the woken farm at its white trades,

He knelt, he wept, he prayed,
By the spit and the black pot in the log bright light
And the cup and the cut bread in the dancing shade,
In the muffled house, in the quick of night,
At the point of love, forsaken and afraid.

He knelt on the cold stones,
He wept from the crest of grief, he prayed to the veiled sky
May his hunger go howling on bare white bones
Past the statues of the stables and the sky roofed sties
And the duck pond glass and the blinding byres alone

Into the home of prayers
And fires where he should prowl down the cloud
Of his snow blind love and rush in the white lairs.
His naked need struck him howling and bowed
Though no sound flowed down the hand folded air

But only the wind strung
Hunger of birds in the fields of the bread of water, tossed
In high corn and the harvest melting on their tongues.
And his nameless need bound him burning and lost
When cold as snow he should run the wended vales among

The rivers mouthed in night,
And drown in the drifts of his need, and lie curled caught
In the always desiring centre of the white
Inhuman cradle and the bride bed forever sought
By the believer lost and the hurled outcast of light.

Deliver him, he cried,
By losing him all in love, and cast his need
Alone and naked in the engulfing bride,
Never to flourish in the fields of the white seed
Or flower under the time dying flesh astride.

Listen. The minstrels sing
In the departed villages. The nightingale,
Dust in the buried wood, flies on the grains of her wings
And spells on the winds of the dead his winter's tale.
The voice of the dust of water from the withered spring

Is telling. The wizened
Stream with bells and baying water bounds. The dew rings
On the gristed leaves and the long gone glistening
Parish of snow. The carved mouths in the rock are wind swept
    strings.
Time sings through the intricately dead snow drop. Listen.

It was a hand or sound
In the long ago land that glided the dark door wide
And there outside on the bread of the ground

A she bird rose and rayed like a burning bride.
A she bird dawned, and her breast with snow and scarlet downed.

Look. And the dancers move
On the departed, snow bushed green, wanton in moon light
As a dust of pigeons. Exulting, the grave hooved
Horses, centaur dead, turn and tread the drenched white
Paddocks in the farms of birds. The dead oak walks for love.

The carved limbs in the rock
Leap, as to trumpets. Calligraphy of the old
Leaves is dancing. Lines of age on the stones weave in a flock.
And the harp shaped voice of the water's dust plucks in a fold
Of fields. For love, the long ago she bird rises. Look.

And the wild wings were raised
Above her folded head, and the soft feathered voice
Was flying through the house as though the she bird praised
And all the elements of the slow fall rejoiced
That a man knelt alone in the cup of the vales,

In the mantle and calm,
By the spit and the black pot in the log bright light.
And the sky of birds in the plumed voice charmed
Him up and he ran like a wind after the kindling flight
Past the blind barns and byres of the windless farm.

In the poles of the year
When black birds died like priests in the cloaked hedge row
And over the cloth of counties the far hills rode near,
Under the one leaved trees ran a scarecrow of snow
And fast through the drifts of the thickets antlered like deer,

Rags and prayers down the knee-
Deep hillocks and loud on the numbed lakes,
All night lost and long wading in the wake of the she-
Bird through the times and lands and tribes of the slow flakes.
Listen and look where she sails the goose plucked sea,

The sky, the bird, the bride,
The cloud, the need, the planted stars, the joy beyond
The fields of seed and the time dying flesh astride,
The heavens, the heaven, the grave, the burning font.
In the far ago land the door of his death glided wide,

And the bird descended.
On a bread white hill over the cupped farm
And the lakes and floating fields and the river wended
Vales where he prayed to come to the last harm
And the home of prayers and fires, the tale ended.

The dancing perishes
On the white, no longer growing green, and, minstrel dead,
The singing breaks in the snow shoed villages of wishes
That once cut the figures of birds on the deep bread
And over the glazed lakes skated the shapes of fishes

Flying. The rite is shorn
Of nightingale and centaur dead horse. The springs wither
Back. Lines of age sleep on the stones till trumpeting dawn.
Exultation lies down. Time buries the spring weather
That belled and bounded with the fossil and the dew reborn.

For the bird lay bedded
In a choir of wings, as though she slept or died,
And the wings glided wide and he was hymned and wedded,
And through the thighs of the engulfing bride,
The woman breasted and the heaven headed

Bird, he was brought low,
Burning in the bride bed of love, in the whirl-
Pool at the wanting centre, in the folds
Of paradise, in the spun bud of the world.
And she rose with him flowering in her melting snow.

In my craft or sullen art

In my craft or sullen art
Exercised in the still night
When only the moon rages
And the lovers lie abed
With all their griefs in their arms,
I labour by singing light
Not for ambition or bread
Or the strut and trade of charms
On the ivory stages
But for the common wages
Of their most secret heart.

Not for the proud man apart
From the raging moon I write
On these spindrift pages
Nor for the towering dead
With their nightingales and psalms
But for the lovers, their arms
Round the griefs of the ages,
Who pay no praise or wages
Nor heed my craft or art.

Fern Hill

Now as I was young and easy under the apple boughs
About the lilting house and happy as the grass was green,
    The night above the dingle starry,
        Time let me hail and climb
      Golden in the heydays of his eyes,
And honoured among wagons I was prince of the apple towns
And once below a time I lordly had the trees and leaves
        Trail with daisies and barley
    Down the rivers of the windfall light.

And as I was green and carefree, famous among the barns
About the happy yard and singing as the farm was home,
    In the sun that is young once only,
        Time let me play and be
      Golden in the mercy of his means,
And green and golden I was huntsman and herdsman, the calves
Sang to my horn, the foxes on the hills barked clear and cold,
        And the sabbath rang slowly
    In the pebbles of the holy streams.

All the sun long it was running, it was lovely, the hay
Fields high as the house, the tunes from the chimneys, it was air
    And playing, lovely and watery
        And fire green as grass.

And nightly under the simple stars
As I rode to sleep the owls were bearing the farm away,
All the moon long I heard, blessed among stables, the nightjars
    Flying with the ricks, and the horses
        Flashing into the dark.

And then to awake, and the farm, like a wanderer white
With the dew, come back, the cock on his shoulder: it was all
    Shining, it was Adam and maiden,
        The sky gathered again
    And the sun grew round that very day.
So it must have been after the birth of the simple light
In the first, spinning place, the spellbound horses walking warm
    Out of the whinnying green stable
        On to the fields of praise.

And honoured among foxes and pheasants by the gay house
Under the new made clouds and happy as the heart was long,
    In the sun born over and over,
        I ran my heedless ways,
        My wishes raced through the house high hay
And nothing I cared, at my sky blue trades, that time allows
In all his tuneful turning so few and such morning songs
    Before the children green and golden
        Follow him out of grace,

Nothing I cared, in the lamb white days, that time would take me
Up to the swallow thronged loft by the shadow of my hand,
    In the moon that is always rising,

Nor that riding to sleep
I should hear him fly with the high fields
And wake to the farm forever fled from the childless land.
Oh as I was young and easy in the mercy of his means,
Time held me green and dying
Though I sang in my chains like the sea.

In the White Giant's Thigh

Through throats where many rivers meet, the curlews cry,
Under the conceiving moon, on the high chalk hill,
And there this night I walk in the white giant's thigh
Where barren as boulders women lie longing still

To labour and love though they lay down long ago.

Through throats where many rivers meet, the women pray,
Pleading in the waded bay for the seed to flow
Though the names on their weed grown stones are rained away,

And alone in the night's eternal, curving act
They yearn with tongues of curlews for the unconceived
And immemorial sons of the cudgelling, hacked

Hill. Who once in gooseskin winter loved all ice leaved
In the courters' lanes, or twined in the ox roasting sun
In the wains tonned so high that the wisps of the hay
Clung to the pitching clouds, or gay with anyone
Young as they in the after milking moonlight lay
Under the lighted shapes of faith and their moonshade
Petticoats galed high, or shy with the rough riding boys,
Now clasp me to their grains in the gigantic glade,

Who once, green countries since, were a hedgerow of joys.

Time by, their dust was flesh the swineherd rooted sly,
Flared in the reek of the wiving sty with the rush
Light of his thighs, spreadeagle to the dunghill sky,
Or with their orchard man in the core of the sun's bush
Rough as cows' tongues and thrashed with brambles their
      buttermilk
Manes, under his quenchless summer barbed gold to the bone,

Or rippling soft in the spinney moon as the silk
And ducked and draked white lake that harps to a hail stone.

Who once were a bloom of wayside brides in the hawed house
And heard the lewd, wooed field flow to the coming frost,
The scurrying, furred small friars squeal, in the dowse
Of day, in the thistle aisles, till the white owl crossed

Their breast, the vaulting does roister, the horned bucks climb
Quick in the wood at love, where a torch of foxes foams,
All birds and beasts of the linked night uproar and chime

And the mole snout blunt under his pilgrimage of domes,

Or, butter fat goosegirls, bounced in a gambo bed,
Their breasts full of honey, under their gander king
Trounced by his wings in the hissing shippen, long dead
And gone that barley dark where their clogs danced in the spring,
And their firefly hairpins flew, and the ricks ran round –

(But nothing bore, no mouthing babe to the veined hives
Hugged, and barren and bare on Mother Goose's ground
They with the simple Jacks were a boulder of wives) –

Now curlew cry me down to kiss the mouths of their dust.

The dust of their kettles and clocks swings to and fro
Where the hay rides now or the bracken kitchens rust
As the arc of the billhooks that flashed the hedges low
And cut the birds' boughs that the minstrel sap ran red.
They from houses where the harvest kneels, hold me hard,
Who heard the tall bell sail down the Sundays of the dead
And the rain wring out its tongues on the faded yard,
Teach me the love that is evergreen after the fall leaved
Grave, after Beloved on the grass gulfed cross is scrubbed
Off by the sun and Daughters no longer grieved
Save by their long desirers in the fox cubbed
Streets or hungering in the crumbled wood: to these
Hale dead and deathless do the women of the hill
Love forever meridian through the courters' trees

And the daughters of darkness flame like Fawkes fires still.

Lament

When I was a windy boy and a bit
And the black spit of the chapel fold,
(Sighed the old ram rod, dying of women),
I tiptoed shy in the gooseberry wood,
The rude owl cried like a telltale tit,
I skipped in a blush as the big girls rolled
Ninepin down on the donkeys' common,
And on seesaw Sunday nights I wooed
Whoever I would with my wicked eyes,
The whole of the moon I could love and leave
All the green leaved little weddings' wives
In the coal black bush and let them grieve.

When I was a gusty man and a half
And the black beast of the beetles' pews,
(Sighed the old ram rod, dying of bitches),
Not a boy and a bit in the wick-
Dipping moon and drunk as a new dropped calf,
I whistled all night in the twisted flues,
Midwives grew in the midnight ditches,
And the sizzling beds of the town cried, Quick! –
Whenever I dove in a breast high shoal,
Wherever I ramped in the clover quilts,

Whatsoever I did in the coal-
Black night, I left my quivering prints.

When I was a man you could call a man
And the black cross of the holy house,
(Sighed the old ram rod, dying of welcome),
Brandy and ripe in my bright, bass prime,
No springtailed tom in the red hot town
With every simmering woman his mouse
But a hillocky bull in the swelter
Of summer come in his great good time
To the sultry, biding herds, I said,
Oh, time enough when the blood creeps cold,
And I lie down but to sleep in bed,
For my sulking, skulking, coal black soul!

When I was a half of the man I was
And serve me right as the preachers warn,
(Sighed the old ram rod, dying of downfall),
No flailing calf or cat in a flame
Or hickory bull in milky grass
But a black sheep with a crumpled horn,
At last the soul from its foul mousehole
Slunk pouting out when the limp time came;
And I gave my soul a blind, slashed eye,
Gristle and rind, and a roarer's life,
And I shoved it into the coal black sky
To find a woman's soul for a wife.

Now I am a man no more no more
And a black reward for a roaring life,
(Sighed the old ram rod, dying of strangers),
Tidy and cursed in my dove cooed room
I lie down thin and hear the good bells jaw –
For, oh, my soul found a sunday wife
In the coal black sky and she bore angels!
Harpies around me out of her womb!
Chastity prays for me, piety sings,
Innocence sweetens my last black breath,
Modesty hides my thighs in her wings,
And all the deadly virtues plague my death!

This side of the truth

(For Llewelyn)

This side of the truth,
You may not see, my son,
King of your blue eyes
In the blinding country of youth,
That all is undone,
Under the unminding skies,
Of innocence and guilt
Before you move to make
One gesture of the heart or head,
Is gathered and spilt
Into the winding dark
Like the dust of the dead.

Good and bad, two ways
Of moving about your death
By the grinding sea,
King of your heart in the blind days,
Blow away like breath,
Go crying through you and me
And the souls of all men
Into the innocent
Dark, and the guilty dark, and good
Death, and bad death, and then

In the last element
Fly like the stars' blood,

Like the sun's tears,
Like the moon's seed, rubbish
And fire, the flying rant
Of the sky, king of your six years.
And the wicked wish,
Down the beginning of plants
And animals and birds,
Water and light, the earth and sky,
Is cast before you move,
And all your deeds and words,
Each truth, each lie,
Die in unjudging love.

Do not go gentle into that good night

Do not go gentle into that good night,
Old age should burn and rave at close of day;
Rage, rage against the dying of the light.

Though wise men at their end know dark is right,
Because their words had forked no lightning they
Do not go gentle into that good night.

Good men, the last wave by, crying how bright
Their frail deeds might have danced in a green bay,
Rage, rage against the dying of the light.

Wild men who caught and sang the sun in flight,
And learn, too late, they grieved it on its way,
Do not go gentle into that good night.

Grave men, near death, who see with blinding sight
Blind eyes could blaze like meteors and be gay,
Rage, rage against the dying of the light.

And you, my father, there on the sad height,
Curse, bless, me now with your fierce tears, I pray.
Do not go gentle into that good night.
Rage, rage against the dying of the light.

PENGUIN ARCHIVE

H. G. Wells *The Time Machine*
M. R. James *The Stalls of Barchester Cathedral*
Jane Austen *The History of England by a Partial,*
    Prejudiced and Ignorant Historian
Edgar Allan Poe *Hop-Frog*
Virginia Woolf *The New Dress*
Antoine de Saint-Exupéry *Night Flight*
Oscar Wilde *A Poet Can Survive Everything But a Misprint*
George Orwell *Can Socialists be Happy?*
Dorothy Parker *Horsie*
D. H. Lawrence *Odour of Chrysanthemums*
Homer *The Wrath of Achilles*
Emily Brontë *No Coward Soul Is Mine*
Romain Gary *Lady L.*
Charles Dickens *The Chimes*
Dante *Hell*
Georges Simenon *Stan the Killer*
F. Scott Fitzgerald *The Rich Boy*
Katherine Mansfield *A Dill Pickle*
Fyodor Dostoyevsky *The Dream of a Ridiculous Man*

Franz Kafka *A Hunger-Artist*
Leo Tolstoy *Family Happiness*
Karen Blixen *The Dreaming Child*
Federico García Lorca *Cicada!*
Vladimir Nabokov *Revenge*
Albert Camus *A Short Guide to Towns Without a Past*
Muriel Spark *The Driver's Seat*
Carson McCullers *Reflections in a Golden Eye*
Wu Cheng'en *Monkey King Makes Havoc in Heaven*
Friedrich Nietzsche *Ecce Homo*
Laurie Lee *A Moment of War*
Roald Dahl *Lamb to the Slaughter*
Frank O'Connor *The Genius*
James Baldwin *The Fire Next Time*
Hermann Hesse *Strange News from Another Planet*
Gertrude Stein *Paris France*
Seneca *Why I am a Stoic*
Snorri Sturluson *The Prose Edda*
Elizabeth Gaskell *Lois the Witch*
Sei Shōnagon *A Lady in Kyoto*
Yasunari Kawabata *Thousand Cranes*
Jack Kerouac *Tristessa*
Arthur Schnitzler *A Confirmed Bachelor*
Chester Himes *All God's Chillun Got Pride*

Bram Stoker *The Burial of the Rats*
Czesław Miłosz *Rescue*
Hans Christian Andersen *The Emperor's New Clothes*
Bohumil Hrabal *Closely Watched Trains*
Italo Calvino *Under the Jaguar Sun*
Stanislaw Lem *The Seventh Voyage*
Shirley Jackson *The Daemon Lover*
Stefan Zweig *Chess*
Kate Chopin *The Story of an Hour*
Allen Ginsberg *Sunflower Sutra*
Rabindranath Tagore *The Broken Nest*
Søren Kierkegaard *The Seducer's Diary*
Mary Shelley *Transformation*
Nikolai Leskov *Night Owls*
Willa Cather *A Lost Lady*
Emilia Pardo Bazán *The Lady Bandit*
W. B. Yeats *Sailing to Byzantium*
Margaret Cavendish *The Blazing World*
Lafcadio Hearn *Some Japanese Ghosts*
Sarah Orne Jewett *The Country of the Pointed Firs*
Vincent van Gogh *For Art and for Life*
Dylan Thomas *Do Not Go Gentle Into That Good Night*
Mikhail Bulgakov *A Dog's Heart*
Saadat Hasan Manto *The Price of Freedom*

Gérard de Nerval *October Nights*
Rumi *Where Everything is Music*
H. P. Lovecraft *The Shadow Out of Time*
Christina Rossetti *To Read and Dream*
Dambudzo Marechera *The House of Hunger*
Andy Warhol *Beauty*
Maurice Leblanc *The Escape of Arsène Lupin*
Eileen Chang *Jasmine Tea*
Irmgard Keun *After Midnight*
Walter Benjamin *Unpacking My Library*
Epictetus *Whatever is Rational is Tolerable*
Ota Pavel *How I Came to Know Fish*
César Aira *An Episode in the Life of a Landscape Painter*
Hafez *I am a Bird from Paradise*
Clarice Lispector *The Burned Sinner
    and the Harmonious Angels*
Maryse Condé *Tales from the Heart*
Audre Lorde *Coal*
Mary Gaitskill *Secretary*
Tove Ditlevsen *The Umbrella*
June Jordan *Passion*
Antonio Tabucchi *Requiem*
Alexander Lernet-Holenia *Baron Bagge*
Wang Xiaobo *The Maverick Pig*